To

OSCAR

From

....

Written by JD Green
Illustrated by Jennifer Naalchigar
Designed by Nicola Moore

First published by HOMETOWN WORLD in 2018
Hometown World Ltd
7 Northumberland Buildings
Bath
BA1 2JB

www.hometownworld.co.uk

Follow us @hometownworldbooks

ISBN 978-1-78553-807-0

Printed in Italy
HTW_PO201809

OSCAR YOU'RE AMAZING!

Hometown World

Oscar is **AMAZING**.

The nicest, smartest guy.

He's **super cool** (and cool kids rule).

It's true! I'll tell you why...

Oscar is so **helpful**.

He gives this mix a beating.

And when that cake's had time to bake,

he'll help out **with**

the

eating.

Oscar is so **caring**.

He's friend to birds and bees,

and **bugs**, and **slugs**, and dogs, and frogs,

and even **cats with fleas!**

Oscar is a **rOck Star!**

Each time he hears a song,

he sings aloud but does not care

if all the words are wrong!

Oscar has a **lovely** smile

that goes from ear to ear.

Just being around Oscar

leaves you feeling full of cheer.

Oscar is a **smart** boy.
Of that I have no doubt!
He pulls the plug and studies how
the bathwater drains out!

Oscar is so **sporting**.

You'll always see him **grinning**.

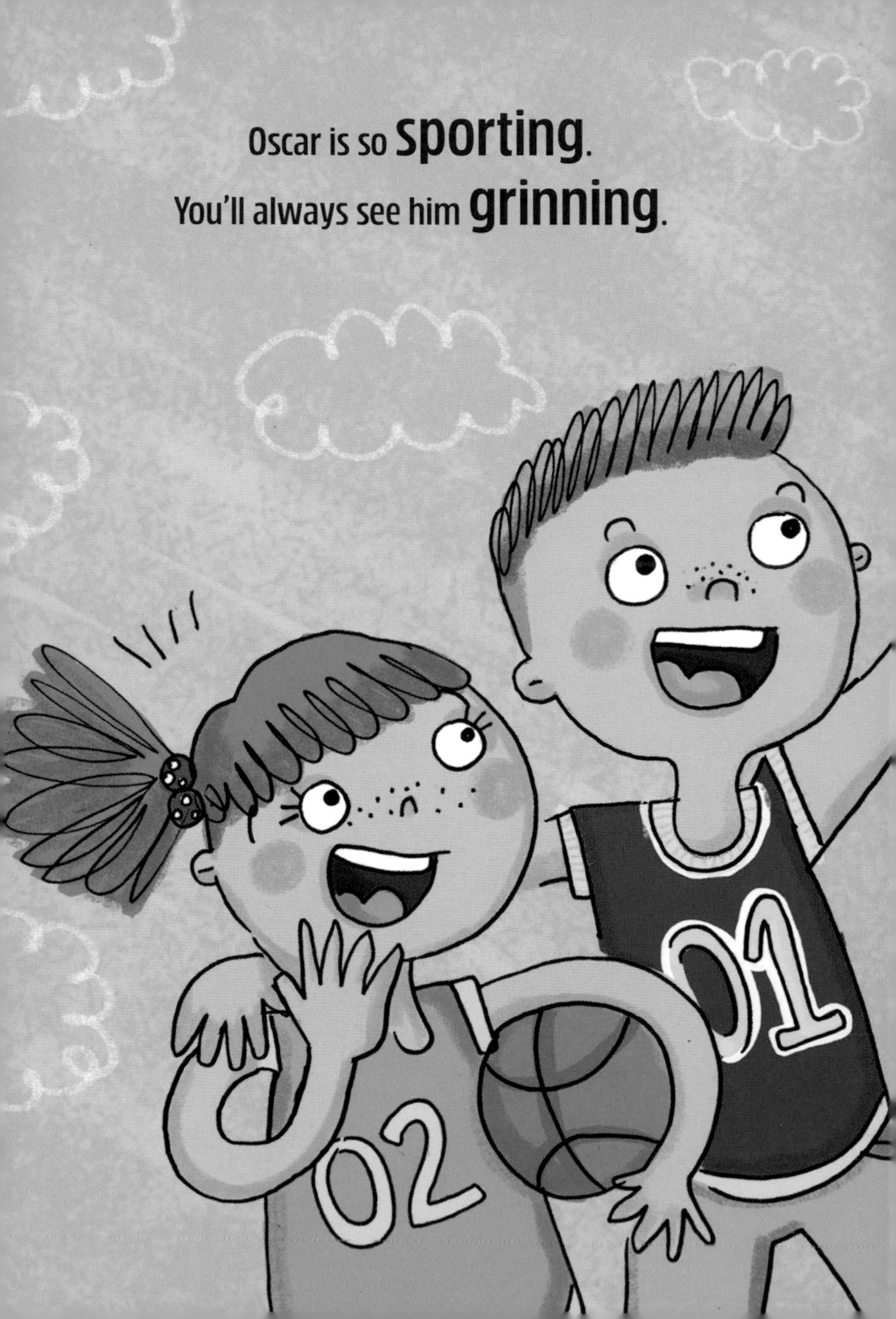

He won't cry if he **loses**
and he won't boast if he's **winning!**

Not **everything** comes easily.

He practises **a lot!**

And that's how he's developed

the **AMAZING** skills he's got.

PHEW!

HEY STANLEY!

Oscar is a
brave boy.

This spider's
not a threat!

He picks it up,
gives it a name

and keeps it as
his pet!

There's always **fun** and **laughter**

wherever Oscar goes.

He likes to dance around a lot

and strike a funky pose...

SO FUN!

Oscar is so **generous**

with all his awesome toys.

He shares them out when playing with

the other **girls** and **boys**.

THE BEST!

Oscar is **AMAZING**.

What sets this boy apart

is that he's **cool**, and **brave**, and **fun**,

and has a ***GREAT***

BIG

HEART!

Add some more AMAZING words about YOU!